This book belongs to:

Zara.

A catalogue record for this book is available from the British Library

Published by Ladybird Books Ltd
80 Strand WC2R 0RL
A Penguin Company

2 4 6 8 10 9 7 5 3 1
© LADYBIRD BOOKS LTD MMVII
LADYBIRD and the device of a Ladybird are trademarks of Ladybird Books Ltd

ISBN-13: 9781846465000
ISBN-10: 1846465001

Printed in Italy

Sleeping Beauty

illustrated by
Anna C. Leplar

A king and queen had a
baby girl. The good fairies
came to see her.
"How beautiful she is!"
they said.

The fairies cast spells
for the baby princess.
"She will be kind,"
said one fairy.
"She will be clever,"
said another fairy.

7

Then, a bad fairy
came in. She looked
at the baby princess.
"How beautiful she is!"
said the bad fairy.

9

Then she cast a bad spell.
"The princess will prick
her finger and die!"
she said.

But then a good fairy cast a spell. "The princess will not die. She will prick her finger and fall asleep for one hundred years."

13

Years went by and
the princess grew
more kind and
more beautiful.

One day, the princess
found a spinning wheel
and pricked her finger.
She fell asleep.

The king and queen
fell asleep, and
everybody in the
castle fell asleep.
Years went by
and thorns grew
on the castle.

One hundred years
went by.
Then one day a prince
came to the castle.

The prince cut down
the thorns and went
in the castle.
He looked at the
sleeping princess.
"How beautiful
she is!" he said.

The prince gave the sleeping princess a kiss and she woke up.
The king and queen woke up, and everybody in the castle woke up, too.

25

"Will you marry me?"
said the prince.
"Yes," said the princess.
So she did!

Read it yourself is a series of graded readers designed to give young children a confident and successful start to reading.

Level 2 is for children who are familiar with some simple words and can read short sentences. Each story in this level contains frequently repeated phrases which help children to read more fluently. Every page in the story is accompanied by a detailed illustration of the main action, which aids understanding of the text and encourages interest and enjoyment.

About this book

The story is told in a way which uses regular repetition of the main words and phrases. This enables children to recognise the words more and more easily as they progress through the book. An adult can help them to do this by pointing at the first letter of each word, and sometimes making the sound that the letter makes. Children will probably need less help as the story progresses.

Beginner readers need plenty of help and encouragement.